Beechwood Review 1

Edited by: Richard J. Heby
Front cover image: *Organic Art #8* by Brandon Glazier
Back cover image: *Flores de Granada* by Ilsa E. Garcia Gonzalez
Cover design by: Richard J. Heby

ISBN-10: 0996624309
ISBN-13: 978-0-9966243-0-5

This book is dedicated to Enid Barry Sonnett.

Table of Contents

<u>Fiction</u>

<u>Non-Fiction</u>

<u>Poetry</u>

Visual Art

Fiction

pages 8 to 46

Shari Crane

A Poet's Five Stages of Grief

Denial:
Receive an email from the "Annual Ipecac Writing Competition." Entertain thoughts of winning. You sent them a good piece; it was revised more often than a realtor's face. Imagine a publishing deal. Imagine handing in your two-week notice. Feel relieved about the prospect of never again staring (while trying not to stare) at that mole with two black hairs when your boss stands over your desk.

Remember the new rule about "no personal emails" at work. Open the email anyway; they'll miss you when you're gone.

"We at Ipecac regret to inform you that the Annual Lavender Sphincter Poetry Competition received a wealth of stellar manuscripts. And yours. However, you will receive a free three-month subscription to Ipecactus, our award-winning online journal showcasing the best writers from all over the globe. Check out the winning entries below. Don't forget to like us on Facebook, and be sure to follow us on Twitter."

Check the email address to make sure they sent the rejection to the correct email. Check again. This can't be. Decide to take a look at the winner's poem, but just to determine where Ipecac went wrong.

The winning poem is capitalized like a psalm and uses "gossamer," "Hyacinth," and "halcyon." Stare. The primary subject seems to be pigeons with "halcyon halitosis." Put on your glasses. The poem's thematic elements explore the social mores of pigeons on leave.

Take off your glasses; they didn't help. Wonder what a pigeon could do, or catch, on leave. Try not to think about it. The winning poem is so abstract you can't decide if the poet is clever or psychotic. Settle on the latter. Hope the poet doesn't live near a park. Open the bottle of antacids on your desk. Eat two.

Anger:
Grind your teeth and resolve never to write a poem about pigeons. Open the bottle of antacids again. Throw two at the wall. Glare at the screen. Read the judge's comments about the winning writer. "Sheer genius and what not."

Check the author's picture, hoping to find flaws—she looks like she eats once per week. Move to her biography, feeling confident. She probably didn't win "Best Halloween Poem" in the fourth grade. Click on her list of publications and awards—it's longer than a DMV line.

Pace around the office trying not to care as you mutter "pushfart" and "tan hooker." Scan for anything that needs shredding. Consider shredding your computer. Set your email filter so anything from that flatulent journal will bypass your inbox and land in the trash. Unlike on Facebook. Unfollow on Twitter. Unsatisfying.

Go back on Facebook. Block Ipecac. Wish the editors were stuck on an elevator between floors with "that one guy" from your writer's group who prefers arguing to revision and eats cheese before group despite lactose intolerance.

Drive home from work in the fast lane. Grouse around in the kitchen. Eat blue corn chips. Check emails at the kitchen table. Finish the bag of blue corn chips. Read an email from "that one guy" entitled, "And Now For Something A Little Difference." Smack your own forehead. Wipe off chip crumbs. He's getting published.

Read your email invitation to "that one guy's" bookstore event. Try to think of a schedule conflict. Your teenaged daughter walks into the kitchen. Attempt to point out the injustice of "that one guy" getting published. Point at the subject line of his email for justification.

Your daughter shrugs and says, "School was easier in the old days." Try to think of a snappy answer as she leaves the room. Watch her leave. Ask the dog, "What are you staring at?"

Bargaining:
Reason that the judge could be unaware she's developing cataracts.

Think about mailing her a pair of bifocals with another copy of your poem. You could offer to accept 50% of the prize money.

Attend your writer's group with two pairs of bifocals. Describe your plan for resubmitting. Use the pink bifocals as a pointer. Ask if you should send Ipecac's judge the pink frames, the polka dot frames, or both?

The group advises against "bifocal resubmission." Feel unsupported. Ask your writer's group if they'd be willing, instead, to request that Ipecac select a different winner? Uncomfortable silence ensues. Suggest if everyone in the group purchased a subscription, Ipecac would be grateful. More uncomfortable silence.

The group advises you to "let it go." Nod, but silently disagree. Think about resending your poem as someone else reads. After group ends, go home and write several witty emails. Delete several witty emails because the group made you promise.

Depression:
Eat chocolate chip cookies. Leave the bag open. Pine about never getting a chance to live mole-free. Pine about going into debt to cover college tuitions. Pine about distaste for abstract poetry. Imagine scrambling the words of your best poem and inserting "pigeon" and "gossamer" randomly to get it published.

Thoroughly investigate Ipecac's prior winners. Realize they have more in common than histrionic poetry—all have an MFA. Calculate the theoretical probability of you receiving an MFA. Use the known variables of teenagers in various stages of puberty, no savings, mortgage, an idiotic ex, and impending college tuitions.

Realize you might get published for the first time when you're 80—if you make it that long. Wear failure like a cape. Eat more cookies. Stare at the wall.

Acceptance:
Remind yourself Virginia Woolf had money, no kids, a supportive husband, and servants. Remind yourself that you have three kids and the only service you get is at the drive-through window, so comparing yourself to others is a feckless hobby.

Think about another way to learn what MFA students learn, preferably without tuition, an advisor with a mole, or leaving teenagers unattended.

Check out all the books on poetic technique at your library. Read both. Decide to purchase used books at a local bookstore. Buy both. Decide to shop at Powell's when visiting family in Portland. Wait three months.

Visit Portland. Ignore dissenting opinions from the back seat about stopping at a bookstore while on vacation. Roam through Powell's like a Rottweiler in a meat factory. Purchase their triple espresso and jack it up with sugar. Have a 45-minute turbo-conversation with another espresso-fueled poet about one poem in Jimmy Carter's, "Always a Reckoning."

Mail three boxes of books home to save on luggage fees. Set five books aside to read while on vacation. After dinner, put your feet up and open a thick book by e.e. cummings. Sniff the pages; think loving thoughts about e.e. cummings and vacation.

Read e.e. cummings critically, looking for technique. Get lost in the poetry and forget about technique. Catch yourself. Frown. Go back two pages. Repeat.

Reading is thwarted by your youngest teen strutting back-and-forth like a chicken to get your attention. Look up from e.e. cummings and watch your son dance. Try not to laugh. Give up on that. Look at the book on your lap and realize you've discarded poetry's joy in pursuit of a benchmark. Plan to write about it—later. Join the chicken dance.

Chella Coutington

The Pond Heron

I can't think of my cousin without seeing the Chinese Pond Heron. Its yellow bill tipped in black. During mating season gray feathers flecked with white turn red. Low-lying, he wades in brackish water, spears a glossy frog. Cracks him in half before swallowing. One leg tucked under his body, he holds position. Behind a break of water palms, silt seeping through the hole in his boot, my cousin holds position too. Waiting for another boy probably his age, fresh from school, handed a Chicom 56 rifle without his asking. They're two seventeen-year-olds, dropped in a skewed world, chins still fuzzy. Eyes too young to detect hate. When my cousin finally spots him, my cousin begins to shiver, nearly loses his grip. The other boy never notices. Caught by the heron taking flight.

Keenan Darnay Clarke

May 14th, 2014

I'm in the Kalahari Desert. It is 13.00 hours and 34 degrees Celsius. It is sub-humid. I am 4663 feet above sea level. The land is a vast expanse of boiling sand, but it is not void of wildlife. The Kalahari sustains wildlife and a fair amount of it per km. My immediate surroundings are quite desolate relative to the majority of the Kalahari and later this evening, I will try and get closer to the riverbank in the hopes of seeing something more than trees.

I have just seen a bird fly overhead, its wingspan looked to be between 1.3 – 1.5 meters. My female instincts are telling me it is a female vulture. It is now in a nest but it looks to be guarding it very heavily. Using my binoculars, I can try and get a closer view of any potential chicks and confirmation that it is in-fact, a vulture. I can't physically get any closer because vultures are known to be unpredictable, especially if they feel threatened. It is not the bird's fault that it does not understand we are here to help its standard of life.

I can confirm it is definitely a vulture, it has a very distinct beak that is only found on this species and there is a nest. I can't get a birds eye view of the nest because, unlike Sir David, they didn't give us camera drones. I think I can see one. Two. Three. Three vulture chicks and the mother, I am told that they don't live in the nest too long because they can be preyed upon whilst being in a vulnerable position and I can confirm that looking at the size of the chicks' heads, that they are not new born. If we are lucky, we may see the vultures leave the nest for the first time. It will have to be soon though, I've been here for 1 hour and 43 minutes now and we're scheduled to go back to camp in 17 minutes at 15.00 hours.

The mother has just flown away and one chick is watching her, it's not objective but, I'd suggest that perhaps the chick is watching her mother fly and is watching her use the energy of the wind beneath its wings to soar and float through space and then the energy within to fly through space, with accuracy and precision. It's incredible and

13

I'm sure the chick thinks the same. She's inspired by her mother, she has to be, it's magical, wonderfully magical and she's still a child so she can still imagine.

She looks like she's imagining flying, she can see herself doing it and she's edging closer. She is literally on the edge. Jump. Or not, she still has doubts, I don't know if she knows deep down if she really wants to do it or if she wants to do it because it's the normal thing to do. Her mum's already done it, her sisters probably will too, unless she makes a stand. Maybe that's what it is and deep down she doesn't want to fly, maybe she just wants to walk or maybe she just wants to be herself. It's got to be hard though, the pressure and the expectation. After all, it is a dessert out there and it's wild and I just feel privileged that I'm here, doing what I love now. I almost didn't love it; I liked the song but I didn't like how it was sang and now, I'm happy. I'm me and I hope when it's time for you to leave the nest, you do so with freedom and passion. It's now 15.00 hours. I don't know if she's going to jump, but I've got a good feeling about it.

Nick Kocz

And One Fair Winter

When the war was over, we crawled out from the bunkers of our ideologies and saw that the sun was bright. Little Ellie, our daughter, ran off to play with children who we vaguely suspected she knew from her preschool class and we were glad that we remembered to bundle her in a cloth coat so she would remain warm. So much of parenting lies in remembering the small things and praying that the big things take care of themselves.

While Ellie played, my wife and I reclined on wicker porch furniture that neither of us remembered buying. We saw our frosty breaths in the cold air, which I irrationally mistook for a sign that death was imminent. My mind filled with anger. Once again, I saw the vile machinations of a homeland security apparatus that jeopardized all that I cherished, and my thoughts leapt to the blogs and listservs on which I could vent my suspicions. My wife, who I'm sure had been much younger in the happier era when we first met, told me that, no, I was wrong, and I feared that she too, like many a good soul in recent years, had gone to the other side.

"It's called steam," she said. Her eyes were blue, with copper flecks, and in the happier era when we first dated, I was confident that she would never mislead me. She could not explain the physics behind our visible breath, but as she spoke, I had the intuition that she was conveying a truth and that however flawed our world may be, it ought still cohere to some greater body of natural law such as she described, so for several minutes thereafter I watched the marvelous thing that she called *breath* float from our mouths.

"But is not death imminent?" I asked.

Purple crocuses peeked through the snow and I smelled the woodsmoke ushering from neighbors' chimneys. My wife put her hand on my shoulder and because she did not instantly refute what I said, I suspected that I was right, that life was just a caesura, a pause before death.

Ellie, god bless her, returned with a snowball. She had lost her earmuffs and her lobes were red with cold. In the time that she had been playing—I can't honestly say how long it had been—she had outgrown her cloth coat and it wouldn't be long before we'd have to enroll her in high school. Let me tell you, there is nothing like the growth of a child to make you realize just how much of your life is slipping away. Somehow she had grown into a young lady with long red hair and a courteous yet happy demeanor.

"It's melting," Ellie said.

The snowball, which moments earlier had been the size of a peach, was now the size of a peach *pit*, and soon it would be reduced to the size of a seed, a kernel perhaps, and soon after that, all that would remain would be the memory of what that peach had been.

"It is one of but many imminent things," my wife said, and though it had been a while, I remembered the question that provoked this response. There would be other wars, other tragedies, and, yes, other financial meltdowns and terror events, but the shadow of immediate crises had passed and we had an interim ahead of us, a vast interim in which we hoped to live the rest of our lives.

The temperature was warmer and all across the land, snow was melting. Red and yellow tulips bloomed in our flowerbeds and it warmed the eyes just to look at their vibrant confident colors, the pinks and yellows, the velvety reds and soft periwinkles. I can't honestly say how long it had been since I last noticed the flowers. My wife looked smaller in her Shetland sweater and it occurred to me that we once talked about vacationing in Ireland before we became too infirm to walk its green hills and see the heather. So much of parenting lies in remembering the small things. Ellie needed to study for her AP Physics class—it's amazing what they expect high schoolers to learn nowadays—but my wife and I sat on the wicker porch chairs and poured glasses of iced tea for each other during that one fair winter when the war was over.

Clyde Liffey
Living in the Moment

Sitting on the living room couch of his moderately well-appointed townhouse last Tuesday morning, Luke was happier than he'd been in months. His starched white pants matched the white of his sofa, his yellow button down shirt gleamed. He had good books beside him, an entertainment system in front of him, and ubiquitous access to the World Wide Web. He picked up the thick book on top of his stack, began reading near where he'd left off the night before. He was just getting engrossed in the narrative – it always took him too long to pick up the thread – when a stray hand pawed the remote. Five people, of various genders, races, ethnicities within and among those races, chatted about markets.

Luke glanced up, lowered the volume. He'd done alright for himself he thought as he surveyed his neatly disordered living room. Though his wife left him soon after their second child was born he had, with little help, raised their two boys – ugly, unathletic, of middling intelligence – to grow into successful men, success as measured by—

The knock on the door derailed his thought. Len, the elder son, entered with his lummoxy gait.

"Good morning, Dad."

"Would you like some breakfast before we leave?"

"No thanks. I ate at the motel."

"Why?"

"It was free."

"Why did you stay at the motel? I had a nice room prepared for you here."

"It was late."

"How late?"

"After eight."

"That's not very late."

"I needed to be alone."

"I needed company."

"I didn't know." Len trudged into the kitchen, poured himself a glass of nearly cold water. Four firm avocados still in their net bag lay on the counter.

Luke replaced his book on the end table. He should have ignored the librarian's recommendation: it made little sense to start a 400-page book he wouldn't be able to complete.

Len sat on the other end of the couch, placed his water glass on a magazine. "I saw those avocadoes on the counter."

"Yes, they were on sale and they looked good. Would you like to bring them back? They'd make a nice guacamole in a few days."

"No thanks. I don't like avocadoes or guacamole."

"That's why you didn't become a lawyer."

"Obeying the laws is enough. Besides a career in finance isn't so bad, is it? If you paid more attention to finances you might not be bankrupt."

"Well, it's over now."

They were silent a while. A commercial for a system that purported to teach math skills came on. Luke furrowed his brow. "Why don't they say what they mean? They're teaching arithmetic, not math."

Len, whose daughter struggled in school, keyed something into his phone. "Maybe they do mean math. They may not know the difference."

"Would you like to see this movie I rented?"

"I probably would but we've got to be moving soon. I have a long drive back."

"I thought you flew."

"No, I drove."

"I scheduled the appointment for a Tuesday so the air fares would be lower."

"I know that but I told you months ago that I was planning to drive. A Saturday or Monday would have been better. I had to take two days off from work."

Luke excused himself, went to the bathroom to freshen up. A thick coffee table book caught Len's eye. He opened it, noticed it was three weeks overdue. Len flipped through the book, a collection of photos of silent movie stars. He stopped at the entry for Douglas Fairbanks, became absorbed in the text.

Luke came back. "I'm ready," he said, startling Len.

"This book is overdue," Len rejoined. "I'll return it on the way back."

Chastened, Luke sat in the passenger seat. "How long is the drive?"

"It should take about thirty minutes."

Luke checked his watch. "I don't have to be there for forty-five minutes."

"It doesn't hurt to be early for once. Besides, I might get lost."

"Going there or coming back?"

"Either way."

They drove along a nearly empty stretch of highway or secondary road. Rather than run the air conditioner, Len lowered the windows. Luke rested his right arm on the car door, exposing a mealy elbow to the world without. He'd forgotten to bring sunglasses. He turned to his left, admired the color his son acquired on his face and on the backs of his hands on the way down, admired too the assured way he drove his owned or rented car.

The land around them was flat. There were no stoplights or other impediments on the road. "Isn't North Carolina beautiful?"

"There's nothing here, Dad."

"Not in this part." They were a long way from the mountains and the coast. "That's the beauty of it."

"It is empty. I'll grant you that. No much opportunity though. That's why I fled to Williamsburg as soon as I could."

"Oh." After a while Luke spoke again. "Why do they have to spell it Centre?"

"What do you mean?"

"With the r before the e. That's not American English."

"I guess they wanted to gussy it up a little, give it a little class. I've seen worse misspellings. Does it bother you?"

"Would I mention it if it didn't?"

"I suppose not."

They turned at a crossroads, headed toward a business district. "I'm nervous, Len."

"Don't worry. You'll come out looking like a champ."

"You'll be there to see me?"

"I can't. I have a long drive back."

They made a few turns, stopping finally on a quiet street in front of the building. All was uneerily calm. They were twenty minutes early. "Can I get you anything, Dad?"

"No, let's just rest here a few minutes."

Len leaned back in his padded seat, closed his eyes, conjured one of his earliest memories. When he was two or three years old, just a cub, his mother — how he missed her! — would seat him on her lap and show him stills of early movie stars. Mary Pickford, he remembered, was his favorite. Or did he just like her name?

19

Somewhere a sparrow sang. He heard the door close, opened his eyes, and watched his father walk caneless with the hobbled jaunty step of a silent movie star down the flower-bordered lane toward the wide double doors of the Euthanasia Centre.

William Cass

I Have a Few

When I was little, my uncle took it upon himself to teach me things. On my tenth birthday, he gave me a puppy, a cocker.

My uncle couldn't speak much English. "Be friend and make responsible," he told me. "Is good."

I had very few friends, so I think his main purpose was the companionship the dog offered.

I said, "I don't think so."

"You try couple weeks. Is not good, I take back."

I guess the puppy and I got along okay. After a few weeks, I named it "Peaches", which was my favorite fruit.

But after a while, I lost interest in it, although I still cared for it most of the time. I scratched its head and let it lay against my feet while I was watching television.

Of course, the day came when Peaches passed away. I was at college when the end was getting near, and my mom called to ask if I wanted to come home; the school was only an hour away. I said I was too busy. She told me later that she and my uncle had buried it in the woods.

~

Once, when I was about thirty-five, I bumped into an old crony named Earl. Our desks had been next to one another's at my first real job, which had been thirteen years earlier, and we palled around together for a couple of years. Then I got a transfer out of the area, which was a bit of a relief because he was becoming needy towards the end. I told him I'd stay in touch, but I never did. I let the emails he sent go unanswered.

Out of nowhere, he pulled in at the next pump while I was filling my car with gas. I saw him, but he didn't see me. I was embarrassed, stopped before my tank was full, got back in my car, and started the engine.

Then I heard Earl's voice say, "Hey, that you, Joe?"

My window was down. He came over and leaned in with bright eyes. He'd lost some hair.

I said, "What do you know? Hey, Earl."

With his fist, he gave me a friendly tap on my shoulder. He kept doing that while shaking his head and saying, "Joe...Joey. Damn, I don't believe it."

We caught up on things quickly. Over the years, as far as I could determine by what he told me, nothing much of significance had happened for him.

He said, "Say, let's go somewhere and get a drink."

I said, "Wish I could, but I have to go."

The truth was I had nowhere special to go, nothing pressing to do. It was a hot Saturday about 4:00pm, the sort of afternoon when even a drink alone would have been refreshing. Instead, I frowned a little watching him in my rearview mirror standing and waving as I drove away.

~

My wife wanted to go to Nova Scotia for our twenty-ninth anniversary. She found a kind of combination guided bus trip and cruise, but we would have had to take a plane and then a commuter train and taxi just to embark on the ship.

She brought it up to me from time to time well beforehand, although she knew I wasn't crazy about the cost and complications. Once, she took advantage of a window-washing project we'd begun together and talked and talked about the scenery we'd see. I just listened and wiped.

Finally, I relented and we ended up going down to a travel agency and talking to a guy who pointed out the unique features of the trip, the itinerary, special meals, things like that. I thanked him and told him we'd think about it. When we left his office, my wife was pretty excited.

Time went along, and I found ways to avoid the topic when she raised it. Eventually, she brought it up less and less, though I'd sometimes find brochures lying around.

When the day came, I gave her a nice red coat instead. She gave me two ties, both of which I wore often to show my appreciation. The brochures went into a folder somewhere, I suppose. She may have thrown them out; I'm not sure.

~

Two summers ago, I was driving down a local rural highway, just after my seventy-first birthday and had become lost. My wife had died, so she wasn't there to help navigate, as I'd grown accustomed. I'd headed out trying to find a farm stand I remembered that sold fresh salt-and-pepper corn, but I couldn't seem to find it.

I approached a car parked on the side of the road that had its hood up. A young woman stood next to the car, a baby balanced on her hip. She turned her head and our eyes briefly met. I pretended to fiddle with the radio dials as I passed, but the radio wasn't on.

I drove on several more miles, thinking, not passing a soul. Finally, I came upon a lonely-looking little diner, pulled in, and ordered coffee at the counter from a big-boned waitress not too much younger than me. I sat stirring it.

After a while, she asked, "You going to drink that?"

I looked up and took a sip.

She asked, "Something wrong with it? Cold?"

"No."

The diner was as empty as those roads had been. She went back through swinging doors into the kitchen. If there were smells, I can't remember what they were.

When she came back out, I asked, "There a garage around here? Mechanic of some sort?"

She pointed. "Bout twenty miles due west. Grangeville."

"That's it?"

She nodded, lifted the decanter, raised her eyebrows. I covered my cup with a hand, paid, and left.

It had begun to rain. I looked back the direction I'd come. Surely the woman had found help by then. Anyway, I wasn't sure I could find my way back. As it was, with the weather, it took me a particularly long time to get home.

~

There are plenty of other incidents of similar ilk. For example, I once reneged on a commitment to buy a horse. I also skipped a nephew's wedding. I never learned to dance. Years go by; time passes. You look around and ask, "How did I arrive at this place? How did I get here?"

I received some sobering news recently. The possibility for a misdiagnosis is practically nil, so I have just so much time left. You can bet your bottom dollar on this: I plan to make the most of it.

Paper on a String

Four things were central to altering the early winter of Jack's fourteenth year, and the first three weren't good.

~

To begin with, at the beginning of December, his father returned from an extended deployment in Afghanistan, one of several recent tours in the Middle East. Along with other families from his military housing area, Jack, his mother, and older sister met the ship holding a banner, shouting and crying and laughing when his father's eyes found theirs in the crowd. The first couple of days after his father got home were fine. They bar-b-qued, went to an amusement park, watched movies; his father even dragged their old remote control monster trucks out of storage and they went down to the school parking lot to race them together.

But then his father quickly turned distant and removed, and spent most of his time sitting on the couch watching reality television and drinking beer. He heard his mother and father arguing from their bedroom late at night. One night, his mother shouted something about his father having a midlife crisis, and then the backdoor slammed and his father's truck roared away. The next morning, his mother told Jack that his father had left to rent a bedroom from a buddy in his unit who had an apartment in a city nearby. His mother stood at the stove frying bacon in her robe with her back turned toward him. She didn't turn around.

~

The second thing happened at school a couple of weeks later. His homeroom teacher, who also taught music, pulled him aside after class one day. She told him that she'd heard Jack singing along to his iPod while he was unlocking his bike from the racks outside her classroom window. She said that he had a lovely voice and that she wanted him to join her school choir the next semester. She told him she'd taken the liberty of having the registrar already add his name to the class list that was posted outside the school's theater.

Some other boys were still milling about the classroom, and Jack was startled to hear them snicker behind him after he'd gone down the hallway to see the posted choir list. When he turned around, one snapped his photo with a cell phone. Two others clapped the photographer on the back and they ran away squealing with laughter.

Later that night, his sister came into his bedroom carrying her laptop. She plopped it down in front of him on his desk and left the room. On the screen was the photographer's Facebook page with the photo of Jack staring wide-eyed into the camera in front of the theater. Next to it was a second photo of the choir list blown up so that his name appeared prominently on it. Below the photos was a single word: "Fag". The post had already been "liked" over a hundred times.

~

The third thing took place right after semester finals and before winter break. His only friend, a boy named Toby who lived a few doors down in housing, came over after school to tell him his family was moving. The military had denied Toby's father's request to stay enlisted as a recruiter after his upcoming retirement date. So, Toby's mother was taking them back to their hometown that weekend for the holidays and so he could start the second semester on time at his new school. He and Toby had spent hours together playing video games. Recently, they'd begun experimenting with creating music digitally and planned on recording some tracks soon. Toby just frowned, gave him a fist bump, and Jack watched their car drive away early that Sunday morning.

~

Jack began spending most of his time either where his father had sat on the coach in front of the television or adding to a list he kept on his computer that he'd titled "Reasons My Life Totally Sucks". Winter break and its abundant free time only exacerbated his feelings. Late in the afternoons, he usually skateboarded down to some warehouses nearby and tried tricks so impossible he knew he'd fall or crash. Sometimes, he skateboarded aimlessly through unfamiliar neighborhoods until he found an empty lot or abandoned building where he could sit and smoke cigarettes he'd stolen from his mother or drink beer he'd taken from the case his father had left in the garage. He often wouldn't come home for dinner. When his mother approached him, he refused to speak to her. His sister treated him with scorn.

The last thing occurred on one of those aimless evening

skateboard jaunts. It was already dark, well past dinner. He turned down sidewalk and saw a piece of paper dangling from the low branch of a tree along the curb under a streetlamp. He stopped to look. The notebook paper was tied to the branch by a string. On the top of it, someone had printed the words: "For whoever lost this money. I found it near the base of this tree." A ten-dollar bill was taped under the words.

Jack stood blinking for several seconds, breathing deeply. He glanced up and down the empty street. A dog barked somewhere, but he didn't notice it. And he didn't notice the breeze that rustled the leaves on the tree. Something began to creep up inside of him, something lost and almost forgotten, and he felt his lips tremble and his eyes fill with tears. They were partly tears of surprise, partly tears of relief, but they were mostly tears of hope.

Andrew J. Hogan

THE TOWEL

The gate swung open, and the visitors entered the old cattle-sorting yard, behind which hovered the old slaughterhouse where Lenny was being held. It had been five years since Aunt Flo's last visit; Uncle Mike had come with her that last time.

The prisoners lined up on one side of the cattle chutes, the visitors on the other. Barbed wired had been added between the side planks to prevent the visitors from touching the prisoners. All exchanges took place through the guards, for a price.

"Aunt Flo," Lenny called. They moved to opposite sides of the chute. "You're looking well." Lenny smiled, but not so much that Aunt Flo could tell most of his teeth were missing. "Sorry to hear about Uncle Mike. I hope he went fast."

"He didn't," Aunt Flo said. "You look like shit. Are you every getting out of here?"

"Not so soon," Lenny said. "Had a little problem with one of the guards. That's actually kind of what I wanted to talk to you about." Aunt Flo stared, silent. "I was wondering, now with Uncle Mike gone, if you might be willing to pass on to me something I could remember him by, his towel?" Aunt Flo continued staring, remaining silent. "You see, there's twenty guys in my stalag, and we have to use the same towel after we shower. We ain't had a new towel in a year or so, and my being sent here, unjustly, for diddling that little girl, well, I get to use the towel last." Aunt Flo still silent. "Well, it's not so bad in the summer when it's warm, but in the winter I'd sure help to have a nice towel like the one Uncle Mike used."

"Well now, Lenny, that towel was one of Mike's favorite things," Aunt Flo said. "I already gave away his other favorite thing, the rawhide belt, to your cousin Pete."

"Uncle Mike told me the 'M' was his initial," Lenny said. "I'd be something for me to remember him by."

"The 'M' stood for the Monarch Motel. That's where Mike and me spent our honeymoon. Uncle Mike stole that towel from the Monarch just for that reason. It's a keepsake."

"Oh," Lenny said. "Don't suppose you've got any other…?"

"Nope. All the other towels are spoken for."

"Okay, I, ah…"

"Well, it's been nice seeing you again, Lenny. Seems like you're making the best of this bad situation."

"Thanks for coming, Aunt Flo. Hope you'll come to visit a little sooner next time."

"With Mike gone, I'm all alone with all the grandkids during the work week, even your little Phyllis. She's growing up real fast, in case you're interested."

"Sure. Thanks for taking care of her. Tell her, her Daddy says hi."

David Chase

Red Shoes

Her fantasy always began with a full tank of gas and $200. She knew she wouldn't get far with $200 but that's where it all started – two hundred dollars and a full tank of gas. If she was in a particularly frisky mood, which happened occasionally, it might also include the red shoes, but they hurt her feet now and they didn't play the role they used to play.

Of course, she could take the red shoes along, just in case, but most people didn't look at her shoes anymore, so it was probably just a waste of time. But then...

See, that's the trouble with fantasies, they get bogged down with details. Who gives a shit about the shoes? Well, there might be somebody. Maybe that would be the key. Maybe in this fantasy she'd actually find someone who likes red shoes. Somehow she associated red shoes as being attractive to men with good hygiene. That would be a change. Okay, she'd take the shoes. And she'd have a full tank of gas and $200. And Dentyne. She'd brush her teeth with Dentyne. That couldn't hurt.

And then she'd drive. The fantasy always involved driving, usually about 100 miles. And on the way there would be this guy hitchhiking – no, no, no, that's not right. Hitchhikers are all creeps and rapists. No, his car would be broken down. He'd be standing there with the hood up and steam would be coming out and his tie would be loose (he'd be a man who wore neckties) and she'd pull over, probably somewhere around mile 75, and she'd say, "Trouble?"

No, no. Jesus. What a dumb thing to say. He'd think she was a moron. No, she'd slow the car until she was just there beside him and ask if he needed a lift. And he'd smile and shrug and he'd put the hood down and grab his jacket before he locked his car and she'd have to move the red shoes off the seat so he could get in. And she'd see him eye the shoes. And she'd say, "I've got a full tank of gas and $200."

And he'd say, "Whoa."

He wouldn't be a talker, either. He'd listen and she'd tell him about her dreams and her family and her job and how she liked to fill the car up with gas, take $200 and her red shoes and start driving, just to see what happened. And she'd say, "Dentyne?"

And he'd say, "Whoa."

And it would be hot in the car, even with the windows down and her hair would be blowing and the currents in the car would make her skirt puff up and he'd notice and she'd pretend it wasn't happening for a few minutes and then she'd "discover" it and put it down and tuck it under her leg so he could see the shape of her thigh and she'd pretend he wasn't watching but she knew he would be so she'd shift in the seat like she was stretching and the seatbelt strap would be between her breasts and make them look bigger and she'd say, "Those are my red shoes."

And he'd say, "Whoa."

And he'd be perfect – big and dumb and stupid. And he'd smell like leather – not harnesses, but good, rich upholstery leather or new expensive shoes and he'd roll up his sleeves because of the heat and she'd see a tattoo of a snake wrapped around his arm with a skull – no, no. Jesus. Not a snake. It would be something like a woman's name on a ribbon around a bouquet. And she'd try to read the name out of the corners of her eyes but it would be too hard to see. She could only see there was a tattoo and smell the leather.

And he'd cough. It would be a clean cough, though, not a phlegmy cough strung with mucous, but a clean cough, the kind of cough people cough before they're going to speak. Maybe it wasn't really a cough. Maybe he was just clearing his throat, or – no, no. He wouldn't cough. He'd chuckle. That's it. He'd chuckle and then he'd look at her and say, "Red shoes?"

And she'd say yes, but she didn't wear them for driving. They were special shoes and she only wore them for special occasions. And sometimes, she'd say as she stretched against the seatbelt again, she brought them along when she felt frisky.

And he'd say, "Whoa."

Isaac Feuerman

A New Apartment

Are these white plates mine or yours? the woman asks. She is stacking dinner plates into large cardboard moving boxes. The kitchen is full of boxes. They are piled everywhere from floor to ceiling. There are boxes in the sink and in the pantry. There is a small box in the microwave. The microwave is in a box in the oven.

Which ones? the man asks. He is sitting at the table on the one chair not covered in a stack of something.

The white ones, the woman says.

There's like three different white ones, the man says.

Well which one's did you bring? the woman asks.

I didn't bring any, the man says.

So they're mine then, the woman says.

They could be Chris's, the man says.

The man opens one of the boxes at the table and looks inside. Where did all of this stuff come from, he thinks. He can't remember seeing the apartment this full when they lived there.

They had lived there for a year. In that time they had made new friends and stopped seeing each other as often. This is just how it happened, they both thought.

Okay, whatever, I'll just leave them then, the woman says.

Well take them if you want, I don't care, the man says.

I don't want them if they aren't mine, the woman says. She looks around. I have enough stuff already.

You might as well take them, the man says. I'll just leave them when I move out.

Why would you do that, the woman asks.

I don't know, the man says. Because they're not mine.

The woman holds up one of the plates to the little crack of light that is escaping the mountain of boxes.

Yea but they are perfectly good plates, she says.

Well then you take them, he says.

I can't. I honestly don't have any more room, she says.

Why don't you ask Jack if he wants them.

She puts the plate back down onto the pile.

Hey, come on. Let's not do that, she says.

Do what? he says. He's probably got some room at his place, it would be a shame to see these plates go to waste, right?

Please don't do this. I'm almost done. Let's just be adults, the woman says.

I am being an adult, the man says.

Great, the woman says.

She opens the refrigerator and pulls out another box and starts piling forks and knives and cheese graters into it.

Eventually she finishes packing everything and leaves.

She comes back the next morning with Jack and they take everything away.

The man hears them but does not come downstairs.

Now that she is gone the apartment is empty.

The man goes downstairs and sits in the living room. The apartment feels small without all the boxes in it.

He goes into the kitchen and finds that she has left him the white plates, neatly stacked next to an empty cardboard box.

He wonders if this was the only box she hadn't packed.

James Stark

A Wartime Wedding-1943

The dress uniform was rumpled. The trouser cuffs ended in the tops of scuffed paratroop boots, hosting sand of some far away land; the tie, tucked into the shirt, had been knotted hurriedly. The jacket, adorned with ribbons and metal signified his war experience at an early age. There was scant time for a smile to shape his sun-browned cheeks, topped by Brylcream-plastered short hair, as the camera flashed, locking in the curtain of trepidation on his prematurely creased face.

She looked to him, hope inscribed on her red-lipped smile and in the sparkle of her green eyes forming pools in her freckled face. Her hair was in a roll around her head, like Rosie the Riveter's. A light-colored skirt hemmed below her knees and a matching jacket, snugged her waist. The picture, the atmosphere, the people and surroundings were monochromatic.

Friends and relatives patched together a reception with a bartered menu from victory gardens, a cake whisked up with eggs from neighbors' chickens and cream from a willing Jersey cow. Greeting time around the tables in the church with neighbors, friends, co-workers and family made short for the abbreviated honeymoon in the spare room of an aunt's lake house. Their brief connubial bliss was interrupted by the dogs of war nipping at the run-down heels of his boots. There was no certainty that it would be resumed.

She would change into coveralls to meet her group's production deadlines as they carefully and lovingly welded and riveted yet another ship to transport him and his cohorts across the ever-expanding vastness.

After this day of promises, embraces, of tears and laughter, of joy, tempered by impending distance and loss, they would proclaim and reminisce their love in censored letters, hers punctuated with crimson lipstick imprints, his with smudged hand prints, smelling of exotic flora.

Food rationing kept rice out of her hair. Instead, confetti from cut-up newspapers describing battles and new armament production fell on their newly-married heads and shoulders. Hand-in-hand they

34

forged a path through well-wishers to the hastily decorated Chevy, powered by officially allocated gasoline. The light brown dust churned from the car's wheels on the graveled road obscured the sun-baked speed limit signs as if proclaiming "hurry" to the couple and participating in their urgency to slake the pent-up thirst for each other. Who knew what would spring forth from those war-rationed loins?

David Gialanella

Cast Out of the Kingdom

In the back of the Greyhound, near the closet-sized bathroom wafting stale odors, three generations sat.

Angela, overstuffed backpack beside her, closed the sociology textbook and eyed her watch. Still three hours to go, and only Aunt Fran's funeral at the end. The vaguely familiar faces of cousins she hadn't seen in almost half her life.

"I'll never keep them all straight," Angela groused, peering over the seatback at the other two. "At least Terry stuck out when he wore the back brace. That's memorable."

"Quit worrying," said her mother, Gail. "They'll have the same problem as you."

"He's straightened up now," the eldest, Rose, chimed in. "Grew into his body."

Angela began describing faces, quizzing the other two on the names.

The bus growled into a downshift as it left the highway for a rest stop wedged between two snow-spotted hills.

"Departing in twenty minutes, with or without you," the driver barked as the passengers emerged stiff and daylight-dazed.

Inside smelled of tinny coffee, frying oil, disinfectant where a toddler's vomit had been mopped. Angela thought about rest stops as great equalizers, scanned for subtle badges of income: shoes, a wristwatch, an insignia. Patrons scurried for the restrooms, cigarettes or aspirin in the shop, foil-wrapped hamburgers columned like soldiers at the eatery. Angela read the labels—single, double, double with cheese—and selected one. A paper cup brimming with fries. One of the diet sodas feverishly poured, capped and set out by a pimply-faced worker.

The cashier, a teenage black girl, sat with a manager looming over her. He poked the register's buttons.

"For the last time, you cannot void an item without me present," the manager scolded, adjusting his glasses. Customers on line fidgeted and huffed. The cashier looked away and lowered the brim of her cap.

Angela's cellphone buzzed with the latest salvo in the text

message skirmish. *Typical woman*, her boyfriend fired, *everythings gotta be on ur terms.* Angela sighed and wondered when they had all become so sensitive.

She watched travelers in the shop eagerly grabbing pop culture magazines, sugary snacks, replacement headphones. Rose wandered among them with arms folded, looking over the bright packages. But only as curiosities—hers was a generation of far fewer necessities.

Angela inched her tray up the rail and remembered to check her surroundings. A janitor's closet, a red exit sign, little cubbies here and there, tables to upend. The kind of thing you needed to consider these days.

She noticed a slender man in a worn sport coat, gray locks down his back, hurry through the main entrance. He marched to the middle of the rotunda, drew not a weapon but a tattered Bible and held it above his head.

"Heed the Word of the Lord!" he bellowed. With his other hand he raised a cardboard poster by its glued-on handle—a paint stirrer.

Angela cocked her head, squinted, recoiled slightly when she made the image out to be an aborted fetus. Onlookers gasped, shielded their children's eyes.

"Disobey the Word and be cast out of the Kingdom of Heaven!"

A man in a stiff white shirt and necktie dropped his half-eaten hamburger, scrambled up from his table and rushed the preacher, seizing him by the collar.

"You have no right," the businessman growled.

"Prepare to bathe in the lake of fire!" the preacher roared, undeterred.

An obese security officer who had been sneaking a cigarette at a service door came bumbling across the rotunda, keys and change jangling, elbows swinging wide around his enormous midriff. Panting, he grabbed the preacher and the businessman, breathlessly mouthing the beginnings of commands.

The shopkeeper, in his threadbare sweater, charged over and attempted to squeeze himself between the businessman and the preacher. The officer tottered, tumbled to the floor.

"Fags and sinners disobey the Word!"

At the money machine, an armored car guard, mouth agape below his bushy mustache, looked back and forth from the tousle to his greenhorn partner.

No, no, no, the partner's eyes pleaded, but the guard bolted toward the fray, left the machine's guts exposed—twenties and fifties lined up in the chamber.

The guard drew his sidearm, had it promptly knocked free by the reeling businessman as the preacher momentarily fought him off.

"Burn!" called the preacher as the shopkeeper dragged him down.

The officer, with the businessman atop him, crawled on his huge belly after the weapon. The guard fell backward over them. The preacher carried on as he lay tangled with the shopkeeper next to the crushed poster board.

"Burn for all eternity in the lake!"

A boxy man in farmer's flannels ran for the pistol but tripped over his own feet.

The men all rose together and converged, grappling anew—the steel slipping, fumbling from sweaty hand to sweaty hand.

The scolding manager swooped in and jumped on the farmer's back.

Two teenagers eyed one another, the exit sign, the money machine, the nervous partner thumbing his own sidearm.

"Cast out!" came the muffled yell from the scrum's innards, the Bible still in hand above.

Another chorus of gasps from the onlookers came. Gail stood near the shop and cried out.

Slow and steady Rose advanced on the pulsating, grunting, struggling humanity, pocketbook under her arm.

"You animals stop that!" she blared. "This instant!"

"Cast out of the Kingdom!"

She came upon them just as the obese officer finally got hold of the pistol and ripped it away from the scrum. His elbow struck the old woman's face with a sharp crack. The men froze and watched her crumple.

Angela helped her grandmother to a table, held a stack of flimsy napkins under the woman's streaming nose. Rose rubbed her swollen knee and stared off. Gail stood crying into her sleeve.

The men glanced sheepishly from one face to the other. Hair drenched, shirts untucked and torn, faces scraped.

Two police cruisers screeched into the lot.

The bus rumbled to life and started rolling.

Zain Saeed

Madeleine Moment Via Found Phone

I was walking along a path in the park. I don't know if I was alone or with her but there were these flowers, yellow ones. I wanted to pick them up and throw them up in the air but there were people screaming nonsensically for no reason whatsoever and jumping about and crying things. I thought I knew her. I know people keep saying this all the time but I lived with her. In the park up ahead she showed me she had put it down somewhere under a bench, and not to tell anyone, God and all. I told her peanuts weren't meant to be used in explosives but she frayed at the edges while she tried to explain to me that there was no way mobile phones could not be charged upside down or maybe something else. I kept insisting we needed to get out of the park and get something to eat but she told me to go sit somewhere near the bench and eat my flowers or was it my peanuts in peace so I did that and I never saw her again. I was sitting there while the bench opposite me began to fly up higher and higher and change colors as it flew and then the people around it began to change colors too. They turned orange or maybe red. But she didn't. She probably didn't. I wouldn't know. Then the people disappeared too. Well at least some of them did – others just decided to lie down and have a little nap on the surface of the sun while the grass shined a bright light on the scene and my face. I had told her I loved her – it was her thirty-sixth birthday and we were going to get wine. The people didn't move you know? The ones that were lying down didn't get up and walk away like I expected. I didn't either, not because I was hurt but because I was waiting for her. I heard the deafening brightness of screaming lights seeing things and I thought about giving her a call but she had my phone.

Charles Bane Jr.

David's Engine

I'll just start at the beginning: when my son was born, I had every expectation that I would leave behind me one day an industrious, kind and well-educated young man who would carry my name. Very few people are remembered for their accomplishments, but a child will remember you if you are loving and supportive. I would be such a father, and the exact same feeling in my wife sealed our marriage like shutters, never overpowered by wind.

Whatever we had to sacrifice to ensure his success, we would do, in the quiet—and to many, unreasonable—compact that parents live by. You see these signatories wearing Timex watches, eying a new car on the Internet, then closing a site's window, buying dress shoes at a thrift shop. Daily, thousands of adult desires stream into savings.

I write of things unseen, because that describes my boy, David. But before I go further about him, remember this: a little boy, and the most remarkable child is still one who must play, be tossed in the air, and carried home. I am so ordinary. But my great comfort is that I was only needed by David to be his father.

It all became evident very quickly. He had taught himself to read at three, within four weeks, and this seemed to be related to an impetus to be able to write. As far as Sarah, my wife, and I could tell, and as far as they knew at his pre-school, he had not employed phonics but simply read whole. It was plain that his true interest wasn't in letters, but numbers and he began, playfully, to multiply two-digit numbers in his head. He only wrote them down to show them to me at bedtime.

He was bored in kindergarten, and the young woman teaching it allowed him to roam the shelves, memorizing the globe, and the star chart she posted (for his benefit) below which he lingered. On a whim, she brought a copy of her undergraduate Principles Of Cosmology for him to glance at. Even for my David, I thought it was too big a leap, when Sarah and I learned of it. We were deeply wrong.

For my son, the discovery of the Big Bang was, I think, a profound emotional relief. He had found his first genuine puzzle. And I thought my child felt an affinity for a rushing cosmos as unbraked as his mind.

I could not slow the spinning galaxies in his head, but I could assure Sarah and myself that the world thirsting to know his potential would not rob him of the normalcy of pizza parties, a dog, and sleepovers. Never mind that he commuted to a junior high school to learn, insatiably, geometry and physics, in the third grade. I refused to allow him to take the math SAT before he was twelve, though I often lay on the grass in the backyard as my son mapped our own stars, and those below our meridian.

When Wesley Schumberger phoned me, asking to meet David, I consented and invited him to dinner. He was perhaps the leading astrophysicist in the United States, and in an academic realm which I had read was fiercely competitive and often petty, he was of a different way, and much cherished, as Louis Leakey had been among his rivals. Schumberger had won the Nobel for his discovery and lucid description of massive black holes at the center of observable galaxies, and the stunning discovery that they affected the speed of stars in a galaxy's outer rim. A super black hole and the life of the galaxy it fired into being were intertwined in fate.

"David," he said in our front hall, "I am Dr. Wesley Schumberger, but since we are colleagues, you are welcome to call me Wesley."

"Would you like to see my room?" David answered.

"Of course," Schumberger answered, and they set off to see David's model dinosaur collection, aquarium, and Hubble posters.

"What a charming dog," Schumberger said at dinner, looking at our Jack Russell. "What is his name?"
"Laika," David answered. Schumberger was shocked, then recovered himself.

"Laika," the doctor said haltingly, "was a dog sent into orbit in the early days of Soviet space flight. He did not survive."

"I know, sir", David said. "I want him remembered."

"Please call me Wesley. David, if I may ask you, what puzzles you the most in your current studies?"

My wife and I served dinner to scientist and son, and ourselves.

David hesitated. "May I ask you some questions? There's no one to ask." I winced.

"Of course."

"Galaxy formation was uniform?"

"That would be my hypothesis, David, but it is unproven. Do you understand?"

"Yes. But each galaxy has within it a super massive black hole? And this black hole is central to the galaxy's creation, and evolution?"

Wesley leaned forward. "It is exactly so, in my mind. What conclusions does this lead you to?"

"I don't want to make a fool of myself", my son said.

"David," Wesley answered, "there are spacecraft, and moon craters named for 'fools'. There is a plot on Mars named for Laika. We forget no one who dares, by enquiry, into the mysteries of space."

"I have a formula I'd like to show you," David said, and wiping his mouth, hurried to his room.
Wesley put a plastic pillbox on the table. "Excuse me," he said to Sarah, "it's that time of day." He had taken his dosages before David returned, and set before him a set of equations.

Schumberger looked at the lined paper, and closed his eyes for a moment.

42

He looked at David, pointing to a letter. "This is a constant?

"Yes," David answered.

There was an utter, beautiful silence at our dinner table.

"The number of universes is..."

"Infinite," David said.

"How could you have known that?" Wesley asked

"It's the answer most generous," David said

"94 billion galaxies in our universe alone," Wesley started. "That's only demonstrative then. I missed that. With singularities at the center of each black hole, in each galaxy, unconstrained by space-time".

"Playing multiple roles," my son answered. "Originators, regulators. My beautiful engines."

Doug Hawley

What?

Duke started hallucinating about a month before seeing a psychiatrist. At 7pm someone, perhaps himself, went flying off a cliff on a horse, but never landing. That was just the beginning. From that day on, each evening at the same time, he would experience what appeared to be a dream overlaying his reality. The next night while talking to his wife Sally, he suddenly saw someone having sex with movie star Vicky Newsome. The male involved looked to be about forty years old, balding and generally pretty ugly. Sally was talking to Duke, but there was no way he could follow what she was saying. "Duke, you looked like you just went into a trance. Do you have any idea what I was saying?"

Duke tried to pretend that he wasn't scared shitless and after a lengthy pause, just said "Sorry, my mind just wandered off for awhile."

Duke was sure he had gone crazy, but was afraid to tell anyone. He just hoped the problem would go away quickly, but no. Every evening, same time, what appeared to be a waking dream would come to him. Sometimes someone was being chased, sometimes it was sex, sometimes it was something that got lost and couldn't be found. Except for an occasional celebrity, there wasn't anyone that he could recognize in his hallucination. There was the one recurring character, the unattractive man who had sex with Ms. Newsome. Rather than admit that he was crazy, he started reading a book at the same time his hallucinations started and just accepted that he wouldn't make any sense of what he read.

After a couple of weeks Duke started to hear a strange voice in his head. He would pick up things like "Its Miller Time" or "I want to go Coney Island." Duke was able to cheer himself up a little because the voice never asked him to kill anybody, not even his boss, who certainly deserved killing.

When the voices started, he broke down and told Sally what had been happening. She tried to reassure him "Whatever is happening, your behavior has not changed at all. Well, maybe your 7pm book habit, but after what you have told me, I can't blame you. Could you have hit your head? I hear that can cause weird brain activity, both hearing and seeing things."

"No."

"Any mental trauma – have you had any shocks or losses that you didn't tell me about?"

"No."

"Okay, I guess you should see a psychiatrist. Keep in mind, as troubling as this seems, we will get to the bottom of it and get you fixed. In case you're worried, I don't mean like we had Kitz fixed."

"That's a relief. Finally, some good news."

Dr. Finley did the standard battery of questions and brain scans, and couldn't find a thing. In desperation, he asked about Duke's hearing aids. "Did you get the hearing aids before or after the hallucinations began?"

"I had them for a month before they started."

"That eliminates my last hope. I can't find anything wrong with you at all. About all I can do is to start you on a tranquilizer and hope for the best."

As soon as Duke started using his prescription tranquilizer the various voices and visions muted, but did not disappear. He decided that he would just have to live with his problem. Neither Duke nor Sally told even their friends or family about what was happening.

A year later, Duke was reading "Popular Science" and saw the article "Telepathy – Fact or Fiction?" He scanned the article until he came to:

"Rumors abound that telepathy devices, which look and act like hearing aides were developed at an East Coast lab. Alleged testing began a year ago last August. It is further claimed that a disgruntled employee of the lab smuggled a sample of the devices into a hearing aid store disguised as a regular set of hearing aids. This all seems to be an urban legend, because the recipients of these special telepathy aids would have reported it by now. The unnamed employee has spread the word that testing began first with dreams starting as the telepathy originator slept from 10pm on, and then started testing waking thoughts."

Duke did some quick calculations. Eastern Time was three hours ahead of his home in Portland. Check. His visual hallucinations started before his verbal hallucinations. Check. The time that the testing started was when he started his visual hallucinations. Check.

Prudently, Duke first saw a lawyer who was entrusted with breaking the news if any harm would come to Duke. After thinking about how much money that he could make writing a book, a little discrete checking around found that it was much easier and a lot more remunerative to sell the telepathy aids quietly back to the lab that lost them. Duke sealed the deal by telling the lab "But wait, there's more – you get my silence along with the devices."

Duke had no more hallucinations, but he did begin living the dream with the money he got. Sally said, "Given how you suffered, I don't think that any amount of money would have been too much."

Non-Fiction

page 48

Anonymous

Chat on the Street

I love Islam, I also love astronomy. Sisters—say a prayer for me.
We will!

Poetry

pages 50 to 94

Darrell Petska

1 Haiku

wintry night
chopping log after log
pine scented sheets

Anne Burgevin

3 Haiku

robin song non-stop mating

first birth
from the narrows
an oriole's song

hummingbird nest
I was once
so small

Ram Krishna Singh

2 Tanka

Peeping through the fog
the sun feebly comforts
a sparrow's nest
built under the windowsill
I hear a new-born crying

Her smile
with the whiff of sandal
makes love livelier.
I search Tao
in the wind's flavour

Bukusai Ashagawa

1 Haiku

I pedal   past
raindrops   pummeling petals
wrung dry   by high winds

Norman Wm. Muise

2 Haiku

torrential rains
the house flooded with
children's laughter

after rain
the playground flooded
with children

Corey D. Cook

birds in a tree

one by one
they drop to the ground –
overripe fruit

Neil Ellman

Ripples

Ripples in the water
how life goes on
a pebble makes
such everlasting waves.

Almila Dukel

The Creek

The creek runs fast
and carries away the fish.
It hides treasures
under the rocks,
behind fallen logs.
Early in the morning
the fog sweeps down to the creek
and greets the fish
in a very polite way

Spring

The woodpecker hammers
to make its home
to lay its eggs in it, too.
The flowers come up,
snowdrops among the first.
Spring will be here
when April comes.
The snow is melting,
the ice is almost gone.
The trees are putting forth their leaves,
and the chickens lay more eggs.
The robins have returned to greet the spring.

1 Haiku

morning dawns
the cat meows
as the fairy sings

Thomas Zimmerman

Mirror

The river's mirror flows unseen, then seen,
breathes mist that honeys tongues and throats in song,
that jewels the threadbare waking mind. The green
and black quotidian grows twelvefold strong
and infinite. We see that everything
is river-fed: the roots and sources, veins
and arteries; the constant flux of wing
and fin and hoof; the spring and autumn rains
that fall on all, combined and recombined.
Our song is crying: jubilation, grief,
the sour-sweet of things alive. We find
ourselves, our place: a baby's hand a leaf,
our genitals in flower, flying geese
the wrinkles in a father's face at peace.

Ann Quinn

Ma

In Japan, Ma is the essential space of nothingness—the empty, the void.

I've been thinking about the in-between
places lately like the space between
words and the silence between notes
and the summer between school years
and the nights between days and how
essential the in betweens are and what
I'm wondering is if death is the in between
space or if life is

Tom Sheehan

Images to Ponder

Just behind the retina,
hidden in a cluster, is a little room
with a secret door and passageways
and key words other
than Sesame.

If you're lucky enough
to get inside that room at the right
time, there's ignition, there's light, there's a flare;
now and then there's pure incandescence
like a white phosphorous shell
detonating, the core room
of memories, the bank

holding everything
you've ever known, ever seen,
ever felt, spurting with energy.
The casual, intermittent presences
you usually know are microscope-beset,
become immediate. For those glorious
moments the splendid
people rush back into your life
carrying all their baggage, the Silver Streak
unloaded, Boston's old South Station
alive, bursting seams, tossing images.

Cabot Trail Liaison

A woman in a blue nightdress
leans on a Cape Breton porch,
steaming coffee in one hand,
the other shading her eyes.

Passing, we acknowledge
her steep privacy, then note,
not yet connected, the lone
sunflower leaning with her.

I Who Lost a Brother

and nearly lost another
remember the headlines, newsreels,
songs of bond-selling, gas-griping,
and movies too true to hate.

The whole Earth bent inwards,
imploding bombs, bullets, blood,
shrieking some terrible bird cry
in my ears only sleep could lose.

Near sleep I could only remember
the nifty bellbottom blues he wore
in the picture my mother cleaned
and cleaned and cleaned on the altar

of her bureau as if he were the Christ
or the Buddha, but he was out there
in the sun and the sand and the rain
of shells and sounds I came to know

years later moving up from Pusan.
I never really knew about him until
he came home and I saw his sea bag
decorated with his wife's picture,

and a map
and the names
Saipan, Iwo Jima, Kwajalein,
the war.

Katarina Boudreaux

Veritas Twice Told

To love

truly

is the only
concept

> right angles, harmonic scales, modulations and
> substantiation, codes, how to boil an egg, how to
> fall down and how to stand up, how to...

that I have
yet

to fully grasp.

Jane Blanchard

for the record

watching you
play baseball
or golf
or whatever
does not count
as a date
in my book

M.J. Iuppa

Hard to Forget What the Heart Asks

Years ago, I was slight enough to slip between raindrops.

Without intention, I worn black Chinese slippers; floated
on light kisses, on steps I wouldn't dream of taking now.

There were doors that opened & closed without a sound.

I slept on blanket hand-me-downs, among hardcover books
open to passages I would learn by the blush of dawn.

Sleep rarely came with dreams; yet, when I awoke, I found
words ink-stained on my palms. I drew figures, women

in repose. I remember thinking that it took such steady
work to be idle.

Like saved postage stamps, it would cost me my life.

Trina Gaynon

Seasons of the Fisherman
--Two Japanese Prints

i. Raise Your Eyes

Red sun rides
low over the mountain slope,
Sailor heed the warning.
Today mend your nets
where cherry trees
bloom on shore.

ii. From Indoors

Powdery
snow, decorative as lace,
lies on bare trees and roofs.
Standing in his boat,
the fisherman
remains moored.

Joan McNerney

Invitation

Would you like to unwind
an afternoon at the lake?

Solar sparks spilling over us
in showers of golden sizzle.

Put on short shorts, skimpy tops,
stick our toes into oozy mud.

Breezes will shake treetops
while we listen to birdsongs.

Why not float on new grass
facing an Alice blue sky?

Read celestial comic strips
from mounds of clouds.

We can count sunbeams,
chase yellow butterflies.

Devour bowls of cherries
painting our lips crimson.

This noontime is perfumed
with millions of wild flowers.

Let's go away all day...be
embraced by the goddess.

Claire Booker

Unpeeled

Freud's having a field day, sharpening
his pencil in that 'train through tunnel' kind of way,
chewing me over with his second best organ.
He scrawls *onion* across my ribs.
But who needs tears on a night like this?
I'm all cock a doodle, riding a Bratwurst so ample
it straddles the plate. This lady's a boy-girl, reeling
in the breadth of it: twitching dowsing stick
and rawl-plug all rolled into one. Hips jut, flip it
just like a fella walking the beast, tight on its leash.
Curious hound, ears pricked, snouting
for the roar of underground rivers.

Walking the Edge

We trail bright verticals pocked with flint,
whiter than yarrow heads, whilst underfoot, lime
insinuates, eclipses my boot seams.

You in your impractical espadrilles uncoil
your charm. I see the pearl in your mouth,
catch a hint of cigarillo.

You gather me in, as I harvest rue for drying –
a fine crop. Your words, I think, will pass as migrant birds:
beautiful for a season, but you will be constant.

Not so – those expert hands have weighed
my flesh, ground these yielding bones to raise
your bread and now you're slaked, you'll drop me

eternally laughing into your eighth collection –
muse an honourable estate: think Lizzie Siddal
to your Rossetti.

Think again.
I'll not be your bricked-in anchorite. I am
the countless beats that stir in this great cliff.

Ryan Meyer

Reassurance

I took the time to try to be human
On a Sunday afternoon at home
In my bathroom while the 'rents were away.
The sunlight from the window touched my skin,
Soft, warning me not to be reckless.
I wasn't being reckless,
I was in the act of reassurance.
The tub was filled with tepid water
Only slightly hazy from the half-assed
Cleaning job I attempted to tackle.
Something about cleaning the smooth
White acrylic felt like I was wiping
The insides of my skull, pushing out
All the caked-on pretentiousness,
The ignorance, and the egregious thoughts
That skated about like whispering imps.
My fingers skated, too, atop the water
And it sloshed against the sides of the tub
Waiting for something to greet, to embrace,
To wrap its warm arms around.
Wanting to think no further,
I plunged my head beneath the surface
And listened to the pulsing of blood
Through my ears, the steady thudding
Of my heart in my head
As it fought to keep my lungs from
Flooding themselves with lukewarm tap water.
In those few moments, before I resurfaced
And sat upon the cold linoleum floor,
There was finally a time when I could
Completely hear myself

Duane Locke

ECO ECHOES 8

"Many things in the old days
Made one popular among his peers:
A sun tan, smoking cigarettes, slinging a yo-yo into the air,
Underage whisky drinking, shaking hips in a hoop,
Saying 'Hubba hubba,' shop-lifting in dime stores.

Son, what makes one popular today?"

"Dad, drug addiction."

"Son,
I found a joint
In your room,
What does this mean?

"It means I now,
Once a loner, have many friends.
Dad, I was just following your advice,
Daddy, as you said
Having friends is the most important thing in life."

Tom Holmes

Scripture

I learned to write watching mother
mow the lawn. Back and forth. Ruling
perfect lanes that her thin shadow marked.
She did this every week – cutting and marking.

Corey Mesler

Odds and Ends

I think a twist of metal is a spider.
I think a spider is the Antichrist.
I think the Antichrist sleeps at my feet.
I think I will live forever.
I find a note to myself written inside
a seashell: There are no odds.
I still believe in odds. I still believe in
ends. I think it's odd I will live forever.

R. Gerry Fabian

Pagan Reactors

The fire dragons
are scattered across the country.
They hide in the mist
of the water they devour.
They taunt the sun
with their potential power.
The small child in each of us
is occasionally visited
by their neutron nightmares.
Tribal leaders convince us
to sacrifice land to them.
Secretly, we all await the moment
when one will spit fire death
high into the air currents.
And so we wonder and watch and wait
in this modern medieval mystery
where the only certainty in plot
is there are no dragon slayers
to save us.

Sylvia Riojas Vaughn

Quonset Hut on the Navy Base

Monsters in the shadows.
Blankets curtain off
cots from living quarters.
A long unlit
way to the back.
Monkey bars nearby,
brother falls,
loses a tooth --
first time I see Mother cry.
Endless hills behind
marked with numbers.
Some kid tells us
it's a practice bombing range.
I make a pickle and mayo sandwich,
stand in the arched doorway
shivering in August.

Doug D'Elia

Dead Babies

From a distance it looks as if
she is carrying a sack of rice,
but it's a dead baby

she'll place at our feet
with sad eyes, and
a ghost of a chance.

As if our magic, our special medicine
could heal its napalm burnt,
shrapnel infested body.

As if we can bring her baby
back for an encore smile or
one last lunge at a beating breast.

As if some Christian missionary
had told her of Lazarus risen,
shaking off both dirt and death.

As if we could pull-off
that kind of miracle,
we can't.

As if seeing her
approach we could murmur
anything other than

Oh, Christ!
We can't. I wish we could.
Jesus, I pray we could.

William Doreski

Painted on a Truck

Could Mao be hiding behind
those brittle rimless glasses?

Could his wire hair represent
no man's land in Mongolia?

Could his missing tooth present
a gap larger than Manchuria?

Could his flaking old complexion
mask a door rusted shut forever?

Could this truck, numbered 47,
park without causing a riot?

Could Mao fail to recognize
a truckload fresh from China?

Will the post-capitalist masses
fail or refuse to salute?

Gary Beck

Landlord Versus Tenant

We went to the Hall of Justice
to request redress
from a callous landlord
who collected rent promptly,
but would not give us
hot water, heat in winter,
maintain the elevator
so my infirm husband,
wheelchair bound,
could get outside
and get back in.
But the judge didn't care,
believed the landlord,
dismissed our complaint,
told us to come back
with petitions from other tenants
so it wasn't just our word
against his.
So we got the other tenants
to sign a petition
and returned to the Hall of Justice
where the landlord claimed
we could have signed the names
and the judge agreed, said:
'Come back with witnesses'.
So we approached our neighbors
who were also suffering
and asked them to accompany us
to the Hall of Justice
and tell the judge
the landlord's abuses.
But before we could arrange a time
the landlord threatened them
with immediate eviction
and they were too frightened

to testify.
Conditions continue to deteriorate.
We can't find an elevator building
with affordable rent.
We can't move to an outer borough,
it's much too far from work,
so we'll try to get the city
to enforce the building code
and compel the landlord
to make necessary repairs,
an improbable hope,
but all we have left.

John Grey

SATURDAY NIGHT IN THE CITY

Filament catches flame
in a party girl's eye,
blind angels see nothing but possibilities,
lovelies step from taxis legs first
as a stumbling drunkard
rotates like a color wheel.
From club to sidewalk,
brightness blinks
equal measure of good life and insanity,
lights fueled with enough brilliance
that any face can be adored,
form a network
of blue-red incandescence
as midnight on the clock,
jerks down the beer lever,
ale gushes as free
as a bartender's advice —
mankind should never be saved from this.
Even people with no cachet
can push the button,
screw in the bulbs.
Every shine has purpose
from a wallflower's pale skin
to a diner's broken sign
to the glitter of the brown canal.
It's not just moths
who dance around the lanterns.

Steve Klepetar

Street Scene: Chelsea, 1981

Manhattan in the rain, streetlights
blur in a sweet, gentle glow, belie

the misery of that cold, wet night.
Umbrellas bump, cabs woosh through

puddles and everyone gets soaked.
Gray buildings rise into a gray sky.

Rain transforms stoplights to fairy
shapes, red and green streak the avenue.

Raincoats mean business as they lean
without faces and swirl into the wind.

The air stinks of ash and worms.
How beautiful, this frozen moment,

opening senses to the teetering brink
of madness and pain and everyday joy.

James Croal Jackson

BICYCLE WHEELS, EMPTY PARKING LOTS

The spokes on the wheels
spoke of hyperspace tunnels
we could fall into forever
suspended in orbits
circling, circling.
We spoke of forever,
how short that is.
Spoke porcelain
bowls smoked joints
made points
in German accent jokes.
Spoke grass tones.
Spoke of bed
dreams of bed
in red made-up languages

we woke we spoke we
never learned we
joked we hoped we spoke
our smokes I watched
you smoke we
sucked lips
(turpentine kissed)
all that time we
spoke smoke we

don't speak of that now

Ally Malinenko

Surgery #2

If you have your period
during surgery
they give you disposable underwear.

And they don't let you use a tampon,
which I found sort of surprising:
trying on a paper outfit
with paper underwear.

I wanted to make a joke
to you about
little Jackie Paper
and Puff the Magic Dragon
but when I see your face

as they wheel in the oxygen machine
to test my respiration before I go under anesthesia

I know that it's not the right thing to say.

I do not know yet,
that this will be one of the last periods
I will have

that in a few months
drugs and injections
will shut the lights off inside me,
board up the windows
wind down the clocks.

But that is still a few months from now,
and I don't know yet
as I stand here
in paper underwear
thinking of just one thing to say,

to make you laugh.

To try and make this okay.

Surgery #3

Okay baby,
the tech says
as I lay topless on the
metal table,

this is going to hurt a little,

and I have to thank him for his honesty
as he slides a needle into the side
of my breast
and again into my nipple.

I know sweetie, I'm sorry,
he says as I wince
and tell him it's fine.

And it is
comparatively
because in the next room
are needles with grappling hooks
at the end
and there I won't be able to lay down
and let the world spin away.

No—in there, they will give me a shot
that doesn't numb anything
and then they will jab and jiggle
until the grappling hooks
find all three tumors
until I'm holding the sides of the machine
just to stand up,

until I'm trying to look these women in the
eyes as they study the screen and not my face
and say, *let's try that again,*
I'm not happy with this one,

before pulling the needle back out

wet and hot with pain
and telling me again,
Allyson,
one more time, okay?
Try not to breathe.

Askold Skalsky

STEEPLE

Between the solar power lab
and the flat rooftops of the office park—
a spire,
   spotlighted,
     white, slim giant needle
as though wanting to puncture heaven
and enter cleanly without a single rip,
pulling behind it the dense indifferent weight
   of glass and brick.

PARADE

I have worn out every argument
and no longer care to be cynical.

Silence will take from me
the words you remember

and file them past you like
a parade of beggars trailing

in the sunshine after some old band
on Saturday afternoon.

That's the way it was, was it?
they will ask.

And I will answer yes,
yes.

Johannes S. H. Bjerg

9 poemwords

condoctor

assadsin

s&diment

earthquack

cumulust

ohsean

dandeliar

operaerratic

refugeese

Visual Art

pages 94–99

W. Jack Savage

I Followed The GPS and Look Where We Are

Eclipse Over Norway

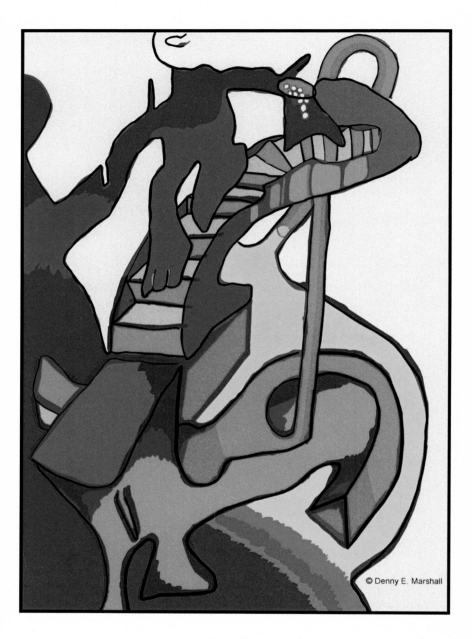

Denny E. Marshall

The Thief

The Portal

Maria S. Picone

Sea Steps

Brisbane Walkway

Thank You

Dear reader,

Thank you for dedicating your time to go through this project of passion. I truly hope that you have enjoyed the moments you have spent with this publication, and that you have gained something from the first issue of Beechwood Review. Whether you have gained entertainment, an emotional experience, or just a few moments to yourself, every experience you gain from reading this publication is yours for as long as your memory will allow it.

If you have purchased this copy as a memento, then please keep it as such. If you have purchased it to share with friends, or have received a free review copy then I implore you to please share these works! Lend the book to a friend, leave it for the next curious patron at a café, or resell it to a random someone across the world. My intention with Beechwood Review is to get the work of these talented artists in front of as many people as possible, and I hope you will support me in that mission.

Kindest regards,
Richard J. Heby

•••

To submit your work, please first read the guidelines in their entirety at beechwoodreview.com/submit then send your work in the body of an email to submissions@beechwoodreview.com. You can direct any questions, comments, or requests for bulk purchase to Richard J. Heby, available at editor@beechwoodreview.com.

For more information please visit: beechwoodreview.com

Thank you!